MEGAMIND

BAD. BLUE. BRILLIANT.

I AM MEGAMIND

PRICE STERN SLOAN
Published by the Penguin Group
Penguin Group (USA) Inc., 375 Hudson Street, New York, New York 10014, USA
Penguin Group (Canada), 90 Eglinton Avenue East, Suite 700, Toronto, Ontario M4P 2Y3, Canada
(a division of Pearson Penguin Canada Inc.)
Penguin Books Ltd., 80 Strand, London WC2R 0RL, England
Penguin Group Ireland, 25 St. Stephen's Green, Dublin 2, Ireland
(a division of Penguin Books Ltd.)
Penguin Group (Australia), 250 Camberwell Road, Camberwell, Victoria 3124, Australia
(a division of Pearson Australia Group Pty. Ltd.)
Penguin Books India Pvt. Ltd., 11 Community Centre, Panchsheel Park, New Delhi—110 017, India
Penguin Group (NZ), 67 Apollo Drive, Rosedale, North Shore 0632, New Zealand
(a division of Pearson New Zealand Ltd.)
Penguin Books (South Africa) (Pty.) Ltd., 24 Sturdee Avenue, Rosebank,
Johannesburg 2196, South Africa

Penguin Books Ltd., Registered Offices: 80 Strand, London WC2R 0RL, England

ISBN 978-0-8431-9922-2   10 9 8 7 6 5 4 3 2

BAD. BLUE. BRILLIANT.
I AM MEGAMIND

by Sierra Harimann
illustrated by Mada Design

PSS!
PRICE STERN SLOAN
An Imprint of Penguin Group (USA) Inc.

When I was just eight days old,
my parents packed me up
in a blue spaceship with my pet fish, Minion.
They wanted me to survive
before my planet was destroyed,
so we set off to find a new planet.

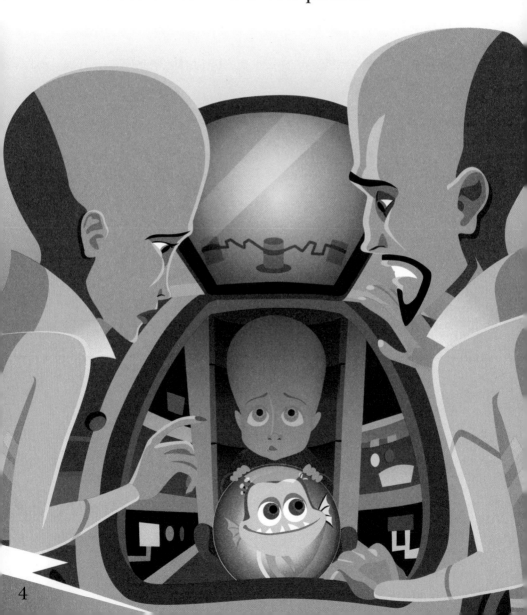

Minion and I were alone
on a bumpy journey to this new place.
Or so I thought.
A golden pod flew right by me
carrying a survivor from another planet.
That golden baby was
enjoying a smooth ride through space.
And when he stuck his tongue out at me
I knew he would be my enemy forever!

The golden baby landed on Earth in Metro City in a good house with good parents. I named him Mr. Goody-Two-Shoes.

I landed in a prison and the inmates became my family. They taught me the difference between right and wrong. I learned that a police officer was bad and a robber was good!

It wasn't long before I met
Mr. Goody-Two-Shoes again.
In school, he built towers of blocks
and I knocked them down!
He received gold stars,
while I was sent to the corner
for quiet time.

The only way for me to win our battles
was to be as bad as I could be.
I developed a skill for building devices
and I became Megamind,
Metro City's smartest villain.

METRO CITY MONITOR

Through the years, Mr. Goody-Two-Shoes
became Metro Man.
He was Metro City's beloved hero.
He had the power of flight,
strength, and great hair.
And he kept throwing me in prison.

METRO CITY
MONITOR

After escaping prison,
one day everything changed.
Minion and I kidnapped
reporter Roxanne Ritchi
in my invisible car.

Roxanne was Metro Man's
number one fan.
She always said nice things
about him in her news reports.
I used her as my bait
to get Metro Man.

Metro Man knew what to do.
We had gone through this same
routine many times before.
I kidnapped Roxanne, he saved her,
and I always lost in the end.

But this time, something went wrong.

I mean *right*!

I succeeded in my plan.

Imagine my surprise!
This time Metro Man was trapped
under a copper dome.
As it turned out, copper was his weakness.
I didn't know that.

Then I blew up the dome
that Metro Man was trapped under.
I had done it!
I had defeated the
most powerful man in the universe!

I had everything, but I wasn't happy.
What's the point of being bad when
there's no one good to try to stop you?
I was bored!

Then I had a great idea.

I would create a new hero,

so I had someone to fight!

I needed someone just like Metro Man.

A speck of dandruff from Metro Man's cape

would do the trick!

It held Metro Man's DNA.

But while I was working,
Roxanne and her partner, Hal,
found my secret hideout.

Then there was a little accident.
My Metro Man DNA capsule ended up in
Hal's nose.
He turned into Metro City's new hero:
Tighten!

Tighten did not know the first thing
about being a hero.
He thought *he* was supposed to rob a bank!
Minion and I had to show him the ropes.
First we put on disguises
so he wouldn't recognize us.
Then we taught him how to be Metro City's
new hero.

Tighten wasn't the best student.
He just liked the attention and the power
that came with being a hero.

This plan wasn't going according to plan.
Tighten was supposed to be the hero,
but he was turning out to be a real villain.

He hurt anyone who got in his way.
And he didn't care if he
destroyed Metro City, too.

Someone had to stop Tighten.
It was time for my backup plan.
I tried to use the copper dome
that had once defeated Metro Man.
But it didn't work on Tighten.

It was time for a backup plan
for my backup plan.
I had to create another hero to stop Tighten.
I needed more Metro Man DNA
so I went to Metro Man's secret hideout.

I didn't find DNA at his hideout—I found Metro Man!

He was still alive.

My old rival had faked his own death.

He had quit being a hero
so he could focus on playing guitar.
Metro Man did not want
to be Metro City's hero anymore.
Instead he wanted to be Music Man!

I realized someone else
would have to be the hero in this plan,
and that someone was me!

After all, there would always
be the battle between good and evil.
Who could do a better job defeating evil
than the smartest man in town?

When Tighten saw me coming to fight him,
he tried to use his strength to defeat me.
Tighten hurled a building at me.
I was knocked out cold.
But I didn't let that stop me!

I had something Tighten didn't have:
brains—and a new plan!
Tighten thought he had knocked me out,
but it was really Minion dressed as me!
That's when I flew in dressed as Metro Man.
I tricked Tighten and defeated him
once and for all.

Megamind: Defender of Metro City.
You know, I might get used to that.